To:""

Happy Reading

!! :)

Patricia Nicholodff

Order this book online at www.trafford.com
or email orders@trafford.com

Most Trafford titles are also available at major online book retailers.

Print information available on the last page.

ISBN: 978-1-4907-7776-4 (sc)
      978-1-4907-7775-7 (e)

Library of Congress Control Number: 2016916526

Our mission is to efficiently provide the world's finest, most comprehensive book publishing
service, enabling every author to experience success. To find out how to publish your book,
your way, and have it available worldwide, visit us online at www.trafford.com

Trafford rev. 10/12/2016

www.trafford.com
North America & international
toll-free: 1 888 232 4444 (USA & Canada)
fax: 812 355 4082

SOPHIA'S YELLOW SCARF

BOOK TWO

PATRICIA NICHVOLODOFF
Illustrated by Shannen Marie Paradero

There above her, caught in the branch of the tree, was the longest yellow scarf Sophia had ever seen.

"It's just what I need," she said with a big smile, "a scarf for my hat."

She carefully unraveled the scarf and then unraveled it some more and unraveled it some more.

Sophia put the scarf across her shoulders, and over her shoulders, and around her neck, and over her shoulders, and around her neck, and over her shoulders. She ran and leaped, and ran and leaped with the yellow scarf floating behind her.

Sophia ran downtown, and all the townspeople loved the long yellow scarf.

"Do you know whose yellow scarf this is?" asked Sophia.

"No," said the townspeople. And everyone agreed that Sophia should keep the yellow scarf.

Sophia loved the scarf too, but there was something not quite right about it. The scarf simply did not match her red hat. So she decided to cross-stitch a red pattern in it.

When she was finished, there were twenty identical diamond shapes down the center of her scarf. Sophia was very pleased with her scarf and went downtown to show the townspeople.

"Oh," said a young mother who was rocking her baby back and forth. "The red diamonds on your scarf look beautiful."

"Ah," said a businessman who was walking to a meeting. "The red diamonds match your hat."

"Well, well," said a mathematician who inspected the diamonds very carefully. "These cross-stitches are very interesting."

Sophia smiled at all the townspeople. "Thank you," she said. "I love the diamond shapes too. Did you know they make all sorts of marvelous patterns?"

"Really!" said the young mother. "Please show us."

"I would absolutely love to," said Sophia, and she got out her palette and paintbrushes and painted some wonderful diamond-shaped patterns.

The townspeople became very excited about the diamond-shaped patterns. They practiced drawing them every day. In fact, everyone loved the patterns so much that they helped one another paint their houses in diamond-shaped patterns.

Soon, ladies wore dresses and scarves with diamond-shaped patterns. Men wore diamond-shaped ties and carried diamond-shaped brief cases. People chatted and served diamond-shaped cookies. And children raced diamond-shaped go-carts all around the neighborhood.

The townspeople even made diamond-shaped kites. The kites floated across the sky from one end of town to the other. Everyone came to join the fun and to see the kites swirl in the air.

The people became more and more excited about the diamond-shaped patterns. And joyful enthusiasm spread throughout the whole town.

But one day, everything seemed to go wrong.

Children came up to Sophia and cried, "Our kites are gone, and we don't know who took them."

Then other people cried, "Look at our houses. Our patterns are ruined."

And a boy cried out, "My go-cart is gone. Sophia, please help me find it."

"Don't worry," said Sophia. "I will find out who is ruining and taking your things."

Then one day, Sophia got a phone call.

"Hello," said Sophia.

"Hello," said the caller. "I am calling to ask you to come to a celebration to receive an award. We are proud of you for inspiring kindness with red hats. And now we are proud of you for spreading joyful enthusiasm throughout the town."

"So," asked the caller, "will you come to the hall for the celebration? The presenters will be a young mother, a businessman, and a mathematician."

"I would absolutely love to!"

"Thank you," said the caller and hung up the phone.

Sophia continued to wear her yellow scarf with the red diamonds. Every day she inspired people to create beautiful patterns. But sadly, some of the patterns were still being ruined. And diamond-shaped kites and go-carts still went missing. Even though Sophia kept a careful watch over the town, she could not solve the problem.

22

Finally, the day of the celebration came. Sophia woke up to get ready, but when she wanted to put on her scarf, she couldn't find it.

Sophia quickly ran downtown to ask the townspeople if they had seen it, but when she got to the town there was no one there.

Then she heard a clapping noise. It was coming from the hall. She ran to the hall and went through the open doors.

Sitting up front with the three presenters was a girl wearing a red hat. And wrapped around the girl was a yellow scarf with red diamonds!

"That's my scarf!" said Sophia, pointing to the girl. "And that's my hat."

"No, it's my scarf!" said the girl. "And it's my hat."

"Wait a minute," said the young mother. "Which one of you is Sophia?"

"I am," said the girl.

"No, I am," said Sophia.

"Please take the hat and scarf off so we can tell who you are," said the young mother to the girl.

The girl took off the hat and scarf.

The young mother said, "The girl standing up front is Sophia!"

"But this is still my scarf," said the girl.

Sophia thought quickly. "If you are the true owner of that scarf, then how many red cross-stitches are in the center row of each diamond?"

"Ten!" said the girl.

The mathematician, young mother, and businessman took the scarf. They carefully counted the cross-stitches.

"Correct," they said.

"Hum," said the young mother as she examined a diamond through a magnifying lens. "How many cross-stitches are in row nine?"

"Nine!" said the girl.

The young mother counted the stitches. "Correct."

"How many cross-stitches are in row eight?" asked the mathematician.

"Eight!" said the girl.

"Correct," said the mathematician. "This scarf must belong to the girl sitting up front."

"Wait!" called Sophia. "Those questions were too easy!"

"Okay," said the mathematician, "then answer this question. How many cross-stitches are in one diamond?"

The people in the audience sat on the edges of their chairs. The girls wrote down their answers on some paper.

Then the mathematician made some quick calculations and looked at the girls' answers.

The mathematician held up his arm to make his announcement.

"Sophia is correct!" he said.

"That is just a lucky guess," said the girl sitting up front.

"Okay then," said the mathematician. "How many cross-stitches are there in all of the diamonds?"

The audience gasped and held their breath.

The girls wrote down their answers and handed them to the mathematician. The businessman and young mother began counting the cross-stitches.

"This is going to take a long time," said the businessman.

"It could take all day," said the young mother.

But the mathematician made another quick calculation.

He looked at Sophia's answer and shouted, "Correct!"

Pointing straight to Sophia, the mathematician said, "The yellow scarf belongs to Sophia."

The mathematician gave Sophia her scarf.

Then he said to the girl, "Why did you take the scarf? You must be the one who is taking our kites and go-carts."

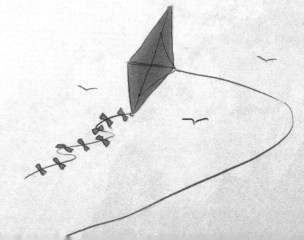

But just then, Sophia turned to the girl and said, "Wait, I want to talk to you."

Sophia went over to the girl and whispered something in her ear.

In a shy voice, the girl said, "Okay."

Then Sophia asked, "What's your name?"

"Laura."

Sophia gave Laura a hug, and a little smile came across Laura's face. The girls continued to talk; and during the celebration, Laura apologized to the townspeople, and all was forgiven.

Then everyone cheered when Sophia announced that she would share her award with the whole town.

Later, at Sophia's house, the two girls cut the yellow scarf in two and made two new scarves.

"Would you teach me how to cross-stitch?" asked Laura.

"I would absolutely love to," said Sophia.

And together, they cross-stitched more red diamonds on each scarf.

The girls put the scarves across their shoulders, and over their shoulders, and around their necks, and over their shoulders. Sophia and Laura ran and leaped, and ran and leaped with their yellow scarves floating behind them.

And the two girls became friends forever and continued to spread their joyful enthusiasm to everyone.

How many cross-stitches are in one diamond?

CPSIA information can be obtained
at www.ICGtesting.com
Printed in the USA
LVOW05s0008031116

511251LV00018B/114/P